# Loon Lake Fishing Derby

# Loon Lake Fishing Derby

written by Kathleen Cook Waldron

illustrated by Dean Griffiths

WORMS
1 DOLLAR
A
DOZEN

ORCA BOOK PUBLISHERS

Loon Lake was a quiet place. Pathways and roads wound like vines around cottages, gardens, and patches of green grass. Everyone enjoyed the peace and quiet.

Everyone, that is, but Mr. Pike. Early one morning he looked out across the calm lake. "This place is *too* quiet," he decided. "What we need here is more action. Let's have a fishing derby."

Mr. Honeycutt looked down at Mr. Martin and nodded. "A fishing derby!" he grunted.

Word spread faster than dandelion fluff in a storm.
Posters popped up everywhere.

Articles and announcements appeared in the *Loon Lake Gazette* and on the six o'clock news.

By Friday afternoon fishermen began streaming into town, towing their boats behind them. Mr. Pike directed the traffic with his whistle.

Across the road, Wally Dale was weeding the garden for his mom. He paused mid-weed to push up his glasses and watch the traffic. "Bait," he thought. "Fishermen need bait. And our garden is crawling with bait. Fat, juicy, fish-delicious WORMS!"

Wally dumped his bucket of weeds and started filling it with worms. Then he printed a sign.

"Gimme a dozen," yelled the driver of a red Chevy, waving his money out the window.

"I'll take two dozen over here," someone called from a blue truck. Robyn, Rusty, and Justin stopped to watch. So did C.J. Nobu followed. Then Kenny.

By Friday evening fishermen were pouring into Loon Lake, all wanting worms. Wally sold worms as fast as he could dig them.

That night Wally found a flashlight, went into the garden, and dug, dug, dug. When he finally fell asleep, his dreams were sprinkled with worms and fish, dirt and dollars.

The fishing derby began early Saturday morning. Mr. Pike was so busy directing traffic that his whistle stuck to his lips.

WORMS
1 DOLLAR
A
DOZEN

Wally went to work as soon as he woke up. He set up a table, put up his sign, pushed up his glasses, and looked across the road. He wiped his glasses and looked again.

Robyn and Rusty had both set up worm stands. Justin handed a man a can of worms and pocketed the cash. Nobu and his four brothers paraded by in sandwich signs, all advertising worms.

By lunchtime Loon Lake was crawling with worm sellers.

NOBU AND BROTHERS WORMS CHEAP

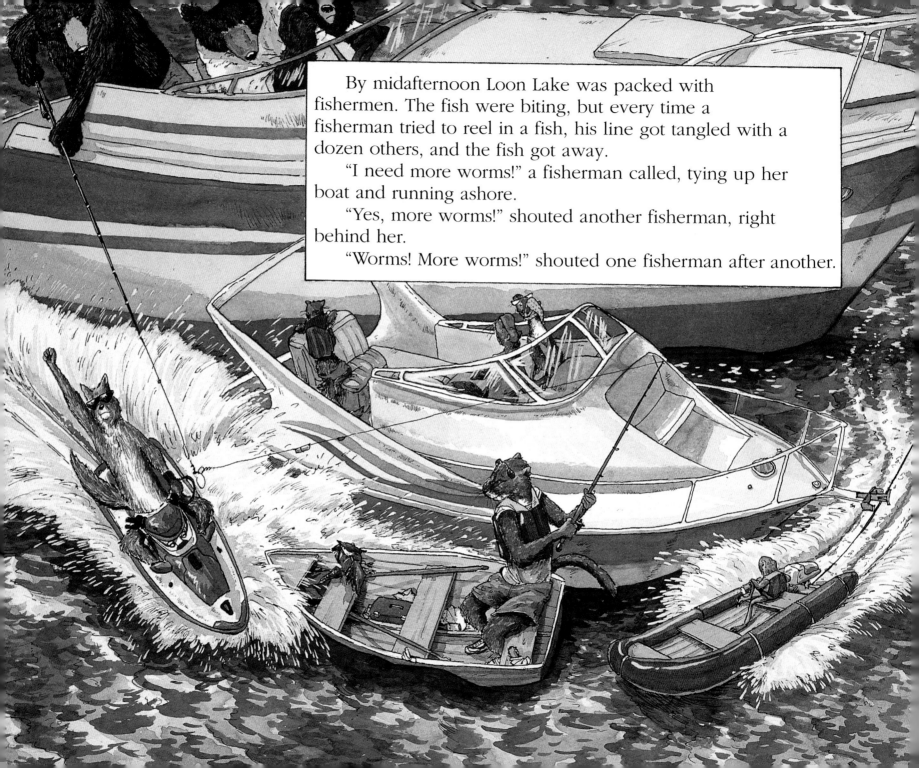

By midafternoon Loon Lake was packed with fishermen. The fish were biting, but every time a fisherman tried to reel in a fish, his line got tangled with a dozen others, and the fish got away.

"I need more worms!" a fisherman called, tying up her boat and running ashore.

"Yes, more worms!" shouted another fisherman, right behind her.

"Worms! More worms!" shouted one fisherman after another.

Kenny punched C.J. for taking worms from his spot.
Rusty and Robyn fought over a sale and ended up
throwing worms at each other. Dogs howled. Cats
yowled. And curses flew over fences.

By suppertime not a shovelful of dirt was left unturned. Petunias and pansies tangled with pea vines, pumpkins, and squash. Mrs. Swift shed salty tears over her carrots. Mr. Martin chased Mrs. Green's cat, thinking it was poor Pooper who had plowed up his pea patch. "Stop," Wally shouted, "STOP!" But no one listened.

That night Wally lay in bed with his eyes open
wide. When he finally fell asleep, his dreams were
splattered with squirming worms and screaming
neighbors.

Sunday morning dawned dry and dusty. Fish, with their bellies full of bait, dove for deep water. Still, fishermen fished — hoping to catch something, *anything*, besides each other. Worm sellers sold their last worms. Mr. Pike wheezed into his whistle. And weary neighbors withered under the hot summer sun, trying to revive their floundering flowers, their drooping vegetables, and their chewed-up lawns.

Wally went outside, picked up his bucket, and headed for the garden. In the coolest corner he could find, he turned loose all his worms. He looked back across the lake at the fishermen frying in the sun. Then he printed over his old sign.

One sunburned fisherman stormed ashore, worm can in hand. As she passed Wally she grumbled, "My mouth is drier than this worthless, wormy can of dirt."

"Wait!" Wally called. "Our garden has just what you need. How'd you like a prize for turning in the first worms — a nice, juicy slice of watermelon?"

He didn't have to ask twice.

Another fisherman held up the biggest worm in his
bait box. "Do I win a prize too?" he asked.
"Sure," Wally said. And he cut another slice.

Word of Wally's watermelon spread like ripples in still water. Fishermen bailed out of their boats and lined up to trade in all their worms. They brought the shortest worm, the fattest, the thinnest, the reddest, the ugliest, the wiggliest — anything for a slice of watermelon.

Wally's watermelon quickly disappeared.

WORMS
$1.00 a Dozen

"I have a watermelon," Mrs. Swift offered, "and my garden needs worms. I'd be happy to trade worms for watermelon."

"So would I," said Mr. Martin.

"Me too," said Mr. Honeycutt.

Mr. Pike tooted his whistle between bites of watermelon, while Wally and the worm sellers helped settle the worms back into the ground.

By the time the fishing derby judges assembled, everyone was chatting and laughing and full of watermelon.

"Since no one caught any fish," announced the head judge, "our prizes go to Wally Dale for turning the Loon Lake Fishing Derby into the World's First Worm Derby. Congratulations, boy."

Wally accepted his prizes. Everyone cheered. Mr. Pike blew his whistle so hard, he nearly swallowed it.

Sunset splashed across the sky as the last of the fishermen
trickled away. Mr. Pike put his whistle in his pocket.

And quiet returned to Loon Lake.

**Canadian Cataloguing in Publication Data**
Waldron, Kathleen Cook.
Loon Lake fishing derby

ISBN 1-55143-142-4

I. Griffiths, Dean, 1967 –   II. Title.
PS8595.A549L66 1999   jC813'.54   C99-910034-3
PZ7.W1466Lo 1999

**Library of Congress Catalog Card Number:** 98-89929

Orca Book Publishers gratefully acknowledges the
support of our publishing programs provided by the following agencies: the
Department of Canadian Heritage, The Canada Council for the Arts, and the British
Columbia Arts Council.

Design by Christine Toller

Printed and bound in Hong Kong

**Orca Book Publishers**
PO Box 5626, Station B
Victoria, BC  Canada
V8R 6S4

**Orca Book Publishers**
PO Box 468
Custer, WA   USA
98240-0468

99   00  01     5  4  3  2  1